Dawn

MOLLY BANG

SEASTAR BOOKS

NEW YORK

SEASTAR BOOKS
A division of NORTH-SOUTH BOOKS INC.

Published in 2002 in the United States by SeaStar Books,
a division of North-South Books Inc., New York.
Published simultaneously in Great Britain, Canada, Australia,
and New Zealand by North-South Books,
an imprint of Nord-Süd Verlag AG, Gossau Zürich, Switzerland.

Library of Congress Cataloging-in-Publication Data is available.
A CIP catalogue record for this book is available from The British Library.
The artwork for this book was prepared by using gouache

ISBN 1-58717-187-2 (reinforced trade edition)
1 3 5 7 9 RTE 10 8 6 4 2
ISBN 1-58717-188-0 (paperback edition)
1 3 5 7 9 PB 10 8 6 4 2

PRINTED IN HONG KONG

For more information about our books,
and the authors and artists who create them,
visit our web site: www.northsouth.com

with many thanks to

Alan

Axel

Betsy

Brown

Bill Cooper

Carol

David

Dawn

Debby

Dick

Dick Sawdo

Dominic

Joan

Joanne

Judy

Leon

Monika

Nancy Fee

Patty

and Willie

"A long time ago, Dawn, before you were born, I used to build ships. Not little sailboats like I do now, but schooners that carried ice and rocks and lumber up and down the coast. I got the wood for the planking from the cedar swamp. Straight and tall the trees were then, not a branch for thirty feet.

One day I was in the swamp when I saw a Canada goose in the water near me. Geese need open space; they should never be in the swamp. The bird had been shot, and its wing was broken. It could scarcely move. I picked it up, carried it home, and nursed it back to health. In a few weeks it flew away.

Time went by. One morning a young woman came into the yard and asked if I needed a sail maker. She was dressed very oddly, with a heavy brown cloak over a dress as pink as your cheeks. She had a long, slender neck and tiny teeth, delicate and white. She had a scar on her arm. I noticed it when she took off her cloak. How could I know what it was from?

The woman said she could sew sails and could weave the cloth for them if there was a loom to work on. It happened I did need a sail maker, but I never thought I'd find one like her. The cloth she wove was the finest and toughest I'd ever seen, and the sails she cut fit the wind like they were born there. The boats would almost fly with her sails.

That was your mother, Dawn. We were married, and before long she gave birth to you. When I saw the pains coming I ran for the midwife, but by the time we got back, you were already born.

I built a sailboat for the three of us, the one that's yours now. When it was finished, your mother brought out a set of sails she'd made to surprise me. I didn't see how she'd made them, but never before had I seen such sails. So light and fine and yet so strong they were that people called them Wings of Steel. All that summer and the next we sailed our boat through the coves and inlets where you sail alone now. How happy we were!

Then one day a man came to the yard. He showed me plans for a yacht he wanted me to build. It was a racing schooner, with the sleekest lines I had ever seen on a hull. He wanted a full set of sails as well, but he wanted sails like our Wings of Steel. Your mother told him no. She said she could only make that cloth once, for us, and she couldn't do it again. The man left, mad as a hornet.

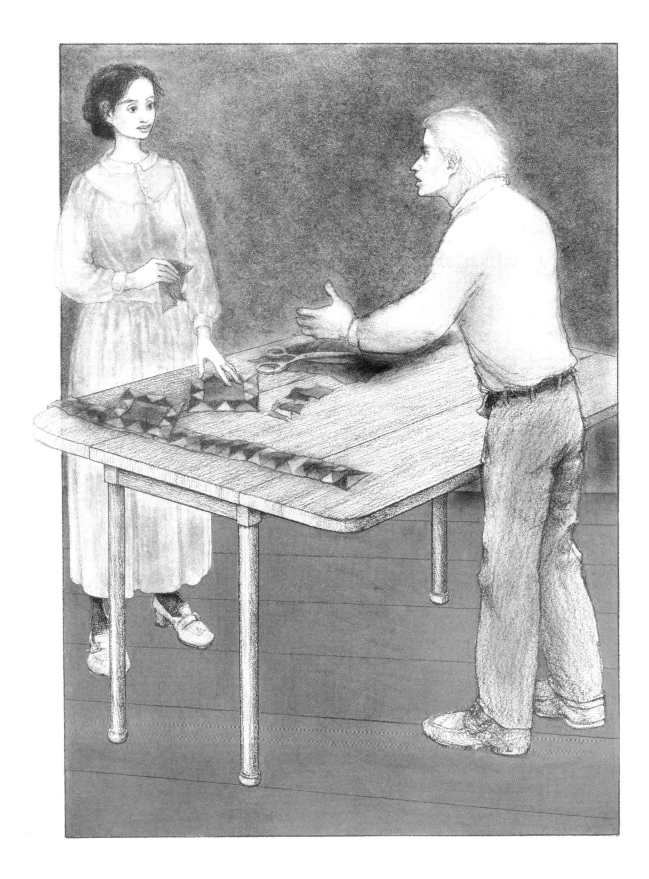

Child, the picture of that boat wouldn't leave me. I pleaded with your mother to make the sails, just this once. She said no, it would take too much out of her. What nonsense, I thought. I kept after her, and at last she relented. She told me it might be the death of her, but I didn't believe her. How beautiful she was then, with her round black eyes and her black, black hair. Before we began, she asked me one thing: never to come into the room while she was weaving the sails. I promised I never would.

The boat was due on the first of August. The two of us set to work, your mother on the sails and I on the hull. You went from one to the other of us, getting into the wood shavings and holding tools for me. I don't know what you did with your mother. Time went by, the boat grew, and the cloth was rolling off the loom as fast as your mother could weave it. But some time in June, she began to get weaker, like she'd said she would.

At last there were only three days left. The hull and all the sails were ready, except the jib. But your mother had slowed down, and it looked like she wouldn't be finished in time. I got angry. I'd never had a job this big, never a racing schooner. I wanted it to be perfect. Your mother told me not to worry, that the sail would be ready by noon of August first. But she would have to work straight until then, and I was to remember my promise and not to come into the room while she was weaving. She looked so thin then. Her dress was scarlet; I thought she'd bought a new one.

One day went by, and the next. Night fell, and she kept working. I put you to bed and lay down myself, and all the while I could hear the thumping of the loom, slow and regular. I got up in the middle of the night and went for a walk. Why am I pushing her like this? I thought. I went to her and called for her to stop, to come to bed, to rest. But all I heard was the slow thumping. I went back to bed, and when I woke up the next morning, I could still hear the loom.

We had breakfast, you and I, and the man came about nine o'clock. He looked the boat over and was satisfied with everything. But he wanted to see the jib. It was the last sail. About eleven-thirty we knocked on your mother's door, but only the sound of the loom answered us. It was working so slowly I could hardly hear it. We went back outside. Finally I couldn't wait any longer. I left you both and went to her room. It was almost twelve. Why couldn't I have waited? I threw open the door. What I saw there, Dawn, I've seen every night since. I'll see it until the day I die.

It wasn't your mother at the loom—not the woman I knew. It was a great Canada goose, who was plucking the last feathers from her breast and weaving them into the sailcloth. All featherless it was—a pitiful thing to see. The goose turned and looked at me, and shuddered.

Suddenly I heard a thunderous flapping outside, and a flock of geese flew into the room. You came in just then, Dawn. Your mother ran toward you with her wings outspread, but I caught her in my arms. She hissed and beat at me with her beak, but I held on. I didn't understand what was happening, you see. I just didn't want to lose her, and I didn't want to lose you either. At last she fell quiet, and I set her down. All at once the other geese crowded around her and carried her off. I never saw her again."

Dawn's father stopped speaking. He looked out at the blue September sky, still and perfect in the twilight.

After a while, Dawn spoke, "I'll bring her back, Father. I'll go in the boat you made for the three of us. We'll be back in the spring, when the geese come north again."

And so she set off.